SOME EYES STILL DREAM

SONAM TOPWAL

Made with ❤ on the Notion Press Platform
www.notionpress.com

This book is dedicated to my mother who has been teaching me since my childhood, the importance of empathy and love towards other living beings, no matter in what forms god crafted them.

Contents

Foreword

She has always been a believer in humanity. Her goal in life is to help others realize what we are here for. I believe we are here to make each other's lives better (the deeds eventually blessed by the supreme lord)

-Vinita Topwal

Preface

This book is a collection of stories of those who are or become unprivileged due to the unprecedented challenges that occur in their lives. Still, they do not lose hope and eventually rise like a shining star.

Acknowledgements

Would like to thank all those who believe that life is a beautiful journey and it glows more when we are together for the betterment of the entire humanity.

CHAPTER ONE

Towards the Cities

Shambhu is a tall, well-built, and intelligent boy of 18 living in the small village of Siroli. Having passed his 12th exam from a govt school situated 8 km away, Shambhu does not want to study further as transportation is a big concern in his area. The degree college lies on the other side of the village where in between lies the jungle area and many cases of animal and men truce and even deaths have been reported. Shambhu scored 90% in boards through immense hard work. Electricity is most of the time not available in his village and drinking water is also a major concern.

His father is a farmer having 2 bighas of land on which a variety of crops depending on the season are being grown. The crops, after being harvested, are taken to the nearby town through a van or a tractor. They are 3 brothers, of all Shambhu is the eldest. Shankar and Shyam could not go to school after the 8th as the distance to the school had to be covered by either an old van, which a man in the village drove to carry the harvested crops or by foot.

Sometimes, he wondered why life in the village was so hard. He had heard of cities with good schools and colleges, well-connected roads, good transportation facilities, and whatnot. He remembers his master saying in the class, "Cities are being revered for what they offer, what are villages to be known for?" To which Shambhu replied, "Sir, villagers require healthcare, and transportation facilities more than anything else. Since, we are solely dependent on agricultural income, it is needed that the crop produced is transported easily and at the same time at least the basic healthcare and education facility is nearby."

To which his master replied, "Yes, most of the people are moving towards cities and towns not for the jobs but for the basic facilities they provide like healthcare, education, electricity, and water availability." Shambhu then asked, "Sir, what can be done to remove this big problem", his teacher replied, "Although govt. is working towards this, but still all the villages in India have to be studied and see that they all have basic amenities for survival. Working on just one or two aspects will still lead to people flocking to the cities and creating a ruckus in those settings.

One fine day, Shambhu decided to visit a city 300 kms away, see the facilities offered, the problems cities are facing and what can be done by us as citizens to address this concern. He purchased a ticket for a train from the station some 20 kms away and boarded for a journey that was about to change everything he imagined.

On his arrival, he saw a huge crowd gather all in and out of the station. With most of the faces being dull and in an anxiety. Roads are full of tea, Manipuri, chole-kulche, pan masala and whatnot, all stalls halting traffic and creating an unhygienic environment. He imagined who were these people, and he asked one of the people, "Why are you selling panipuri on one of these busy roads?" He replied, "There is nothing I get except this as I am only 8th pass. He again asked, "Why have you come to the city?" The person replied, "My village does not have basic facilities of healthcare, water, electricity and transportation and therefore, through just the cultivation of crops, one cannot survive."

He got the same answer from most of the so-called stall owners. He observed within a few days that such a huge population that resides in cities is not living a decent lifestyle, instead, most of them live in rented apartments and struggle hard to meet day-to-day expenses. This may be probably due to lower salaries and wages and the job insecurity they suffer. The lower salaries in the companies are due to the immense availability of people ready to work at a lower salary. He realized that most of them even come from villages and small towns.

He finally understood that in cities, the problems are the same as in villages as people are not earning much in cities due to the huge availability of workers ready to work at very low salaries. He thought, that even though I could get admission easily to a govt college in the city, the question is whether I will get a job with a decent salary. He thought he would create awareness through teaching regarding what is to be done and practised by people to resolve this problem in between and after completing his graduation

CHAPTER TWO

Struggles of Poverty

With the entire city shivering in the cold, Kusum is sitting on an old plastic chair kept in front of a wooden table that she purchased 2 years ago from the earnings of tuition. She is preparing for her upcoming board exams. To be away from cold, she covers herself on the lower half with a small woollen blanket. "Boards are just two months away" exclaims a voice nearby. It is her mother Janki, who wakes up early in the morning, at around 5 AM, and does all the household chores by 11 AM to start her work of tailoring. Govind Nagar is a small village in the big city and the ladies around the nearby houses, usually come to stitch suits and blouses.

Last night, as usual, her father who occasionally gets small contracts to build houses nearby, came and started a drama that has become an inevitable part of her life. How much alcohol can destroy families, who else knows much better than her? "The school will no longer keep Girdhar," "They have been asking for his pending fee for months" shouts her mother. "There is no money, borrow or get out of this place" he exclaims.

The house is an old building, its walls are not whitewashed for ages and the floor is in a dilapidated state. The rent is still too high for them to afford. Whatever her father earns, he spends on buying alcohol. Life has been miserable for them since childhood. Kusum started giving home tuitions in her 8th class and whatever she earned, spends on meeting daily household needs. She and her brother study in a nearby government school and still struggle to pay the minimal fee of the school. Being a bright student, Kusum has even won scholarships.

On a fine evening, her brother asks her, "di on the other side of this street are beautiful houses, who lives in those houses?" to which she gently replies, "Those who do a lot of hard work" to which her brother replied, "We also do so much hard work, then not why we." She said, "They are the ones who earn a lot of money too," Her brother asked, "How can we earn a lot of money.?" She replied, "We have to study well and get a good job." She became a little numb and thought, which is the most challenging task.

Kusum studies from 5 AM till 8 o'clock in the night after which it becomes almost impossible for her to study as her father comes in a drunken state and hurls offending words and this even ends up in domestic violence. In the daytime, she gives home tuitions to around 10 students nearby. A child with so much disturbed surroundings feels mentally harassed and even wants to escape. One day, her father came in the daytime, announcing, "I will not work anymore, if these kids come to this home" "They create so much chaos and even ask for snacks." "Baba, please don't come when I am teaching." "These kids have an exam in the coming month." To which Nathuram, replied by pulling a child's collar and even pulling him away. Her father, who bought himself a bottle of rum purchased on credit from a shop nearby responsible for turning the Mohalla into a "nashedi." Went to the kitchen poured the drink into a glass and started drinking, students witnessing all sorts of drama.

How important it was for Kusum the money she earned from the tuition, she and her mother only knew. "Who will come to study, if the situation is such", she wondered. Thankfully her father did not often come in the daytime and she could continue with her teaching and run her livelihood. She always thought of having a decent and comfortable life but even knew how tough the challenges ahead lie. One fine day, she asks her mother, "Can't the liquor be banned"? Her mother shows a sarcastic smile and says "Then also it would be readily available as demand for the addiction can't die".

Kusum, even after being in a disturbed state of mind, studies hard for the entire two months and gets admission to one of the good colleges. She feels a bit satisfied but college being quite far from her home becomes her plight and her dream of getting a decent job is still quite far. She must still work a lot. She cannot regularly attend college as to bearing the travelling expense, she must teach the students. History, Geography and Polity have become her solid strengths now. She soon realizes her dream of attempting the civil service. In the college library, she finds all sorts of books, related to the prestigious examination. Reads the syllabus, and is stunned by the variety of topics and subjects. On one fine day, a call comes from her house, asking her to come soon as there is an emergency. She asks the reason but does not get an answer. She hurriedly packs her bag and when she arrives sees a picture of her mother nearby with a mala on it. She cannot stop crying. She asks her brother, "How did this happen" Her brother replies, "Father hit on her head with a bottle of rum when she was stopping him from drinking." "Where is he" she retorted. He said, "He is nowhere to be found, police are after him."

Her only support system is now no more. Her eyes became so red with the pain of losing her mother and the anguish she had against her father. She exclaims, "What will I do now?" Life came to a halt and fell unconscious. She saw her mother in her dreams, who was holding her hand and taking her to a beautiful home. She told her, "You will be a beautiful place." When she becomes conscious, her mother's last rites are almost performed. Her brother returning home asked, "Di, how are we going to survive now." To which she replied, "Do you know, maa came in my dreams and said, we will be in a beautiful place soon."

She packed her bag and went to the college the other day, sat for 3 hours in the library reading topics that were part of the syllabus. I would be eligible in the last year for the exam, she thought. Till then, she will be well prepared and will not face problems in attempting the paper. Those 3 years, were painful as her support system had gone. Her brother was now in 12th and to meet the daily expenses was a sheer problem. She started tailoring work side by side to increase the income and her brother helped her by giving home tuitions himself. In the final year, she fills out the form and attempts the prelims well. After one month, when the result comes, she scores a decent score and qualifies to the mains.

With mains being 2 months away, she starts working on the subjective part but due to the vast content, she is not able to prepare the entire content. However, she attempts the paper and waits for the result. 2 months pass and she eagerly waits for the result and finally, when the day arrives, she goes for a prayer in a nearby temple. Comes back and finds, that she qualifies with a rank in the top 10. She goes into a state of bliss and sees her mother delight. She prays, God, please give me the blessing to serve my nation with honesty and help me in creating awareness regarding the importance of being a good human.

CHAPTER THREE

Life on the hills

Well, life in the mountains is both a heavenly and daring experience. I was last week travelling to one of the remote villages of Tehri to see my related family members and on the way toward the village, found a huge waterfall, which seemed like a fountain flowing from heaven. I was spellbound by its giantess. I came out of my small swift given as a gift by my father on my birthday and slowly went nearby and drank some water from the gushing stream formed from its soothing water. I would say, the taste of nature is the sweetest one. On the way, I saw a hill that looked like a bird with its body wearing lovely deodars and oaks. The hills are majestical, the painted blue sky with the yellow colors of sunlight, the cool breeze giving the freshness of a young bairn playing outside with a lovely bunch of friends, the entire view of hills and the waterfalls and the trees, are far from being explained in words.

Finally, I reached the lovely village at around 1 PM. The love with which I was greeted, I can only say, that Pahadi people are true from the heart. For lunch, was offered the rais and toar daal along with rice and bhaangjira chutney. "You have become so lean my son", my uncle said lovingly. "The life in the city is so busy that one to even take out time for food", I replied. To which he said, "Even people in the villages are busy throughout the day in mainly agricultural tasks but still they follow a routine and give ample time for having what gives the energy to work." I wondered, how right he was.

People in the city have forgotten the importance of what has to be done and when. It was 3 PM and I thought of going to the nearby river and observing the flow and giantess of mother nature. One of my cousins, Rohit was purely a mountain boy, for he knew every length and breadth of areas even very far off. He could even tell on what soil, a type of crop could be cultivated, and at this point, which area would be receiving rainfall and how crops would be affected. The Pahadi santra, giant walnut trees, the unending deodars, majestic waterfalls, and every nook and corner were described as can only by the son of the lord of mountains. Rohit has recently been engaged in a mining activity conducted in a nearby village for extracting a rare stone called "soapstone". The blasting of the mountains creates an atmosphere of suffocation and presents a bleak picture of inhumane human activities.

One day Rohit and I planned to visit a place known for the beautiful flowers around. On reaching the spot, I was mesmerized by the variety of flowers. From the germaniums, begonia's, fuchsia, marigolds, hydrangea, it seemed the entire heaven came in front of our twinkling eyes. I asked Rohit, "Do they grow on their own? Or someone regularly waters them?" to which he replied, "Brother, this is the magic of the mountains. God waters them." I said yes. This is only possible with the love of the mother nature. We observed the serene view and Rohit immersed me the popular stories of the Himalayas. He said, "Once lord Shiva came to this place to find out the upper part for his son, lord Ganesha and he saw a baby elephant nearby suffering from some disease who was about to leave the world. On seeing lord Shiva, he asked lord to give him the life of his devotee as human in the next birth to which lord shiva replied, "Your curse is over now and soon you will be born in a family of a famous saint and will be known as one of the greatest devotees of lord shiva."

One day Rohit did not come back from his work. Everyone was waiting eagerly for his return as he was to bring along with him some fresh Khubani's, Plums and Litchi's from the garden of a nearby relative's abode. Dusk has arrived. The swift noise made by the trees due to the cool breeze passing them, could be heard. The howling of some wild animals gave giving a frightening feeling.

Everyone one anxious and waited eagerly but there was no sign of Rohit. His father was continuously trying to reach his number but it was switched off and he seemed to have one else also. He then decided to go to that place where he was nowadays working but as it was dark and wild animals were hovering all around, his mother asked him to call a driver living in the nearby village. The driver reached at 9 PM and Rohit's father and I drove off to the Kinjani village.

On reaching nearby, a major landslide halted our stressful journey. It seemed the landslide happened in the evening. While nothing was visible in the dark, we turned on the torch and mobile phone lights to see the things around the site. On the other side of the road, under the debris, my uncle saw a hand coming out. We were numb and could not utter a word. We slowly moved towards the other side to see. It was Rohit under the debris. We somehow with the help of the driver, managed to take him out but found out he was no more.

CHAPTER FOUR

When I met her

I stay in a beautiful town full of vibrant young minds aspiring to make a change. Hema who is my neighbour has become a good friend of mine as it has been almost 2 years since we have been here. We go on vacations together, hang out at nearby places and enjoy every moment to the fullest. Although all our thoughts match, there is only one difference. She belongs to a state where women are still considered a burden, as she says and I to an abode of gods, the Himalayas. We both are teachers but being a teacher in govt. college is entirely a different thing from being a teacher in a private college. It is not only about salary but the treatment of employees which matters. There is no job security.

From ancient times, a guru has been given the respect that he deserves by even the most powerful kings of all time but in today's world, a teacher is considered nothing more than a person appointed to fulfil endless tasks. Sometimes, I ask myself, why is this happening and then get an answer, which of course everyone knows, If I do not work, several others are willing and at a much cheaper salary. But I try to contemplate, is population only the reason or is it the skill that I lack for not being able to deserve to work for a government degree college? Although I have appeared for many interviews, I have not been able to clear any since I qualified for the National Eligibility test two years ago. Hema, who has just come from a nearby shop asks me, "Have you tried this latest flavour of Chips?" "It's yum." To which I say, "What's different in this"? I ask. "It's coated with green chutney made from cucumber and cottage cheese." "Just try" I find it very tasty.

Hema wakes up at 5 AM and finishes off all the household chores before going to the office. Her mother is a heart patient and although she has two younger brothers, they are of little help. She cleans the entire house, cooks food for all, and washes everyone's clothes before going the college, every day. She hardly gets any time to study in the morning. Whatever she studies is after having dinner. I ask her to live in a PG so that she can get time for herself. To which she replies, "Who will take care of her mother if she is not here?" Life is indeed very tough for her as not only does she work all by herself but also continuously admonished for not being able to earn more even after so much qualification. She sometimes asks me the solution to which I usually do not have a reply.

I sometimes suggest her to get married off for which she replies, that the dowry demanded is so high that her parents say, we cannot afford it. So, the only solution is that she should get a government job. Hema is a brave girl; she always says that I will survive this battle. I will come out as a winner one day. We both discuss each other's stories and laugh out loud to bring some relief in our busy and stressful personal lives. I have shared my side of the story as well with her. Although my life is far better than hers, the main concern is the non-achievement of what I always longed for. Yes, I longed for a decent salary, a stable job and to be a successful teacher and writer. Although, teacher I have become, but not a successful person. Everyone in the family continuously pressurizes me for marriage but I try to make it clear in my mind that I want to work for a career where I can bring a positive change in everyone's life by making them aware of what challenges we face and what could be the solutions. I believe marriage will stop me from that. Since it is not easy to get a job in a college, I feel perturbed. Also, after marriage, my dream of writing can remain unfulfilled due to my busyness and involvement in daily chores.

I every day pray to God, please listen to the pain and agony of a teacher, and make their lives respectable and better. Because only a happy and content teacher can produce ignited minds. As APJ Abdul Kalam once said, "The purpose of education is to make good human beings with skills and expertise. Enlightened human beings can be created by the teachers."

CHAPTER FIVE

What is my Varna?

I have been living in my village since I was born. Surrounded by beautiful hills covered with deodars, oaks and sesame, the valley looks like a majestic blessing of the mother goddess. "Sugar and tea are over," my mother tells anxiously from the kitchen. To which I replied, "We will get it from Manohar's shop" My mother said, "His shop is temporarily closed as he has been out of town for some time now due to his treatment of thyroid and there is no one in his family to look after the shop" Manohar's shop was the only one destination for the people of our village. Rest, all the villages were quite far. I decided to visit the closest village without asking my mother.

When she went to the fields to harvest freshly grown green vegetables, I set off. After a by-foot journey of almost 45 minutes, I reached the small shop in the village of Sampri. I asked the shopkeeper, "Chacha is the sugar and tea available?" to which he replied, "Yes, but who are you?" "Never seen you before," He asked "Tyey Papa naam kya Ch.?" I told him "Shyam Mahara" He first gave me a deep gaze and then said, "Who gave you permission to enter this village?" "Get out" he shouted. A person of the same village standing nearby said, "Don't do this, give the boy what he wants" To which the shopkeeper replied, "Why are you favouring him? He does not belong to our caste" To which he politely replied, "We belong to a caste of humans, and god has created this, so who are we to decide where we belong" I was deeply affected by this man's wisdom and asked him his name, "What's your name Chacha?" He lovingly said, "Beta Shyam Bartwal" The shopkeeper did give me what I asked but asked not to visit this village again.

Shyam Chacha asked me to come with him to a nearby place as he wanted to tell me something. I said, ok" He told me, "Beta do you know what is the most beautiful thing in life"? I asked what is that Chacha, "He said, Mother Earth and do you know why"? I replied, "Maybe it is because it gives us every to survive" "Be it food crops, home, water, air and so on" He politely said, "Yes, it is one of the things, but the real beauty of mother earth is that it sees everyone equally" I thought yes. He was very right. He continued, "Have you ever seen a tree asking, don't pluck my fruits or a stream of water shouting, don't come near to drink my water?" I said "No, never" he further said, "It is we humans who have created differences" "The Varna system of the Vedic period, divided the society into 4 sects the Brahmin, Kshatriyas, Vaishyas and the Shudras. This just meant, if I was a knowledgeable person, I was called a Brahmin or if I involved myself in the trade of goods and services, I was known to be a Vaishya.

This had nothing to do with birth, one was known for what he did or practised." He continued, "The Varna system later turned into caste which can be said to be one of the saddest things that happened in Indian History. I replied, "Yes, Chacha, one should be known by what they do, not through their caste which was created to prove one sect superior to others." He replied, "Yes beta, the only way we can prove that Karma is eventually what matters is by making people aware of this beautiful line, "Karma is the Varna."

CHAPTER SIX

Why am I a refugee?

It is not that my country has less pure air, water, or soil. It is beautifully woven by Mother Nature but there is one grudge that I have against her, why did it give its humans an oppressive mindset? Can't we stay together in peace and harmony? History has witnessed that conflicts have only brought with them the destruction, not only of their homes and lives but even their minds. A country hit by a war whether internal or external, suffers for unending generations. From the last few years, I have been hearing from all around that a truce has started between two groups of the same religion in some areas of the western parts of the country. Although I belong to the same religion, I somehow do not belong to that group, it is the 3rd one that I am from. How does it matter? I keep hearing in the news that these groups have even formed their organizations to gain control over the country's political system. My mother, sitting in one corner of the room, says, "What is the government doing?" "It has been so many years and still they have not been able to mutually settle this" "If this goes on, soon our entire country will be at war"

I even follow the news of other countries, and see that although small truces happen from time to time, the government manages them effectively and the entire country eventually remains united. But in our country, why is the government failing? What is it that separates us from those countries? In search of this, I decided to turn on the pages of the history of one of the most beautiful countries, where multiple religions co-exist and where I have even had an opportunity to stay for a few months during an official visit.

Yes, it is India, the land where lord Buddha, lord Mahavira, and famous saints like Adi Shankaracharya were born. They taught the importance of peace, unity, and brotherhood which I must say has to be learnt by oppressive mindsets working today in the society.

When I was in India around 5-6 years ago, I tasted various north and south Indian dishes, tried to sing with those people, wore their beautifully knit dresses, and most importantly laughed with them knowing no one was to judge me unlike here. While turning the pages of a book that I purchased when I was there, found that although India witnessed many plunderer attacks from believers of other religions and some of them even ruled the country, but they could not change the identity of the country, i.e. its belief system which lies in its Hindu Philosophy. Rulers of other religions did rule the country, but India always remained Indian.

I wanted to understand deeply how Hindu Philosophy became so powerful and realized that this might be found in the epics of this great religion which taught unity and love of humanity. Bhagwad Gita is one such text which teaches the real dharma. Lord Krisha is the leader of the dharma yudha which took place between the Pandavas and the Koravas, millions of years ago. Bhagavad Gita teaches when one faces challenges and problems in life, how one should act or behave. Lord Krishna beautifully says Krodhadbhavati samohah, sammohatsmrtivibhramah. Smrtibhramsad buddhinaso, buddhiansatpranasyati. Meaning, from anger there comes delusion; from delusion, the loss of memory; from the loss of memory, the destruction of discrimination; and with the destruction of discrimination, he is lost. He also taught, yada yada hi dharmasya glanir bhavati Bharata.

Abhyuttanam adharmasya tadatmananam srjany aham. This means, that whenever and wherever there is a decline in the religious practice, O descendant of Bharata, and a predominant rise of the religion- at that time I descend myself. Yes, Lord Krishna taught what eventually became values and has immensely helped in the unity and peace of the country. It is not that other religions' texts do not teach this but the values and principles have been reiterated in different situations by lord Krishna in such a beautiful way that entire humanity can get inspired. Although there has been no founder of Hinduism, the texts and the epics have given such a strong message that even the invaders had to live in peace with this religion.

CHAPTER SEVEN

Towards the Reality

Swati is a young girl of 18 and has just entered her college years. Although, she tried for NEET entrance but could not clear it and therefore was admitted in the B.Sc. course. She has even made many friends in college. "Swati, let's go to watch a movie today" said Shikha who was sitting just behind her and found it difficult to focus on the lecture as she believed that studying microbiology makes her feel like a virus and protozoa herself. Simran who was sitting beside Shikha also said, "Yes, there is this movie on the life of a college student and I have even heard the reviews. People say it is an amazing one." All three agreed and decided to bunk the lectures today.

"Let's click some pictures," said Shikha while they were on the metro on the way towards the theatre. Swati said, "Ok, but I was not prepared for this and therefore will not look good in the photos" To which Shikha replied, "Even we were not prepared, but we all are looking decent enough for the pictures" She said "ok". They were clicking pictures like a recorder records music. "Don't forget to post it on Facebook and Insta," said Simran. All said, "Yes, it would feel great." In 15 minutes, they reached the theatre and were mesmerized by its glorious structure.

There was a huge open space in front where there were counters of popcorn, fries, Nacho chips and sweetcorn. The place was decorated with paintings of all those stars who are even remembered today for their immemorable characters. Also, in between there was a small artificial fountain from which sparkling water came as if the sweetened water came from heaven.

"Let us take some pictures of everything here. So that we do not miss anything," said Simran. Almost six months had passed in the college and Swati was a little anxious as semester exams were around the corner. Guys, "Let us go to watch the movie as we have already taken many pictures and even have made many videos. I think this is enough." "What happened Swati? We have come for some fun and entertainment today so why do you take tension," said Shikha.

Swati replied, Semester exams are about to start and we must study also" "Are, there is a lot of time left, entire 20 days, we will study easily." Simran said. "Let us have some sweetcorn. It seems tasty" Shikha said. All agreed and after holding the cup full of tasty sweetcorns, wanted to again take pictures. So, they took pics from every angle.

"Only five minutes are remaining for the movie to start" Swati said in an alarming tone as they were yet to start what they bought. They hurriedly finished off and went inside the theatre. Lights were off inside the theatre and they could only see the big screen on which some recent advertisements of jewellery, mobile phones and pan masala were running. "Can't we take photos inside the theatre?" Simran said in a low voice. "No, photos not allowed hoarding was placed near the entrance," said Swati. Shikha replied, "This is not fair" "The movie was wonderful" Swati said in a joyful tone and all the others agreed. While coming back, they were again clicking the pictures and posting the same on social media platforms describing each of their activity.

Occasionally, they started venturing outside by bunking the lectures. After the semester exams were over and when the results were out, they managed to just pass the exams. They had developed the habit of focusing on the irrelevant things and therefore the concepts taught in the class were also not clear to them. One day, there was a seminar on this topic on their college campus, and I got an opportunity to explain to the youth, where they are going, what is it they are focusing on and what they should do now. The youth has become distracted and smart devices and social media have played a major role in this.

We always think of posting everything we do so that we get known by others. In this race, others also follow us and through this chain entire youth has deviated from its real path of happiness and achievement. It is not that we should avoid fun but there should be a limit for all we do and it should always be secondary. Our priority should be the attainment of what we desire to become and even after its achievement, we should make other goals for our further success. I believe, that by keeping your real aim in mind, no matter whether you are in a hill station, a movie hall, or a marketplace, nothing will ever be able to distract you from your real aim.

CHAPTER EIGHT

Some Eyes Still Dream

Arjun has been living in an orphanage for the last 2 years. His life drastically changed when his mother and father died in a bike accident. After living with one of his uncles for around one year, he chose to live on his own. The question was where to live. Arjun was 14 and somehow had continued his studies with the saved money of his father but now, the money was almost over and he also had to live alone. He wanted to live on rent but knowing the expense, he decided he would have to live in the underpass nearby and simultaneously search for a job. After 20 days, one shopkeeper agreed to keep him but on the condition that he would get nothing more than a meal three times a day. He agreed as all the money was over and he has been even begging for some time now.

It was a huge grocery store where every household item was available. Every person living in the nearby area visited, as the prices offered for daily consumption items like rice, pulses, wheat, sugar etc; were comparatively lower than the other shopkeepers around. Nathu Gupta was a well-built man of around 30 years and did not like any delay in measuring and packing. One day, while Arjun was measuring 5 kg toor day for one of the customers, the polybag slipped off his hand and the pulse split on the floor. Arjun was admonished badly by Nathu and was asked to leave at that moment. While crying badly, memories of his mother cooking the food came in front of his eyes.

He remembered how one day, while she was making chapatis, he went to take a freshly made one and how it slipped from his hand. His mother said, to Arju, "Take another one, keep that on one side, would feed it to the birds." He started weeping more and, on that day, he even could not have a single meal. He slept without food. The underpass was at a place where hardly anyone came as there was a foot-over bridge nearby so most of the people used foot-over to cross the busy road of Saharanpur. Nathu went off to sleep and, in the dreams, he could see his mother and father blessing him and saying, "You are a strong boy, although life is tough for a small soul like you, but the more you struggle, the more you shine."

For a small boy, who was now on the streets, what could be more important than getting three times meals in a day? He started exploring the area in search of work. Somewhere, he could see the shops of halwai, and grocery, and somewhere there were numerous stalls selling chole kulche, pani puri, tea and whatnot. He asked everyone if there was work and everyone denied saying we were alone enough for this small work. There was a local railway station nearby, when he entered the station, he saw a passenger train coming to a halt and some of the passengers coming out. This was the first time; he saw a train in life. He thought he might get some work here as people regularly flock out and demand certain food items during their journey. Nearby, there were two stalls one selling tea and rusk and the other puri sabji and raita. He asked the owner, whether, there was any work. Both denied saying there was already a helper with them.

Within 50 meters, he saw a permanent shop where chips, water bottles and other ready-to-eat items were displayed. He asked the shopkeeper, please give me work, sahab, my mom and dad have died in an accident and have been living on the streets begging. Have not eaten even a single meal from yesterday. Please, Sahab, I will never forget this favour in my entire life. The shopkeeper first gazed at him for a few seconds, then asked, "Don't you have your relatives who support you" to which he replied, "Yes many, but no one is ready to bear my expenses. I lived with one of my uncles for a year, but I was treated like a person from another planet and therefore decided to leave." "Hmm. I see" he further asked, "Did you go to school before"?

Arjun replied, "Yes, my father worked in an iron and steel factory and we could afford to go to a private school then" The shopkeeper said "ok". "What is your name? "Arjun" he replied. "There is an orphanage, around 100 km from here. It would be better for you to stay there as you can continue your studies." "What is an orphanage Sahab"? "It's a place where those children who have lost their parents live" Arjun further asked, "What do they do there"? The owner replied, "They get a place to live, 3 times meal and the most important a school to study."

Arjun thought something and replied, "Are there such places in the world" The dark and pale shopkeeper replied, "Beta, the love of mother and father is irreplaceable in the world but yes you will at least get the basic facilities and you have to search for love in them." Arjun agreed. The time for closing the shop was around 5 PM and after this, both started the journey towards a new home of this small soul. The train was full of passengers and it was almost 45 minutes journey from there.

Finally, they reached at the gate of the Vivek Sansthan at 5:50 PM. It was an old place will some of the walls in a dilapidated state. The guard stopped them and asked, who they wanted to meet. The shopkeeper said, "The child has to be admitted to the Sthan" Both went inside and saw a huge statue of Swami Vivekananda. On the old walls, there hung many quotes and sayings of wise men. There was a big garden outside the Sansthan with a variety of flowers and trees. There were dahlias, marigolds, jasmines, and roses of multiple colours leaving a smell refreshing the entire mind and soul. Arjun saw some of the children playing in the garden. He could easily relate with them as they were in a similar stage as he was in.

The supervisor of the sansthan came and asked the reason for their visit. They told him the reason to which the supervisor replied, "We admit a child only after verification. So, the child's identity proof and mother and father being no more proof is what we see before admitting the child." The shopkeeper asked Arjun whether he had any such proof. Arjun said he got an ID card from the school he studied in but as far as his parent's proof is concerned, he did not know whether anything existed. The supervisor said "The parent's death certificate has to be submitted so that a valid reason is there with us to keep the child." The shopkeeper asked Arjun, "Beta, your relatives might know about this"

Arjun replied, "Yes. They completed the cremation and other rituals. But I doubt they will make it to this place with the proof." "Do not worry you can visit them and ask them for help. They would have no problem with you living in the sansthan." said the shopkeeper. The supervisor interrupted, "It would be better if one of your relatives visited this place and gave the confirmation with the proof of their death. Till then you can stay with the school's ID proof. We will take the child to the relative's place shortly for them to be here for verification." The shopkeeper said, "OK" He asked Arjun to take care of himself and assured him he would visit as and when he had the time. The shopkeeper left and the supervisor took Arjun to one of the rooms in which four children of his age group were already staying. There were four cots and one fan which was spreading immense air in the warm weather.

Two days later, his uncle came with the proof of Arjun's parent's death. Arjun was quite surprised as he could not understand how his uncle came to know about his stay. He came closer and greeted him with a namaste and a sarcastic smile. A young child with shattered hopes of staying a happy and peaceful life could be seen in his eyes. "Arjun, I got to know about your stay through the supervisor of this place as I received a call yesterday night. Without a delay, I rushed to this place for your safe future. Anath Ashram's is a great place as you get all the facilities as with mother and father." Arjun nodded as he had now understood the bitter realities of this world. After the verification, he went to the common room shared with four others without bidding goodbye to his uncle as he did not want to cry anymore in search of hope

CHAPTER NINE

Why do they stop you?

My office is a beautiful place with well-maintained interiors, the walls have photos and quotes by some of the most well-known leaders of all time. One of the quotes by Swami Vivekananda, which has always inspired me since childhood, "Arise, Awake and stop not till the goal has been achieved" is inscribed just in front of my cabin. Rashi, Aman, and Rakesh are my colleagues as we report to the same manager. "Swati, we have a meeting at 3 regarding the ongoing marketing activities. Sir has asked to convey everyone." I said "ok."

I started reading about all the platforms and media we are currently using to promote our IT products and how successful they have been in turning up sales for our organization. A person suddenly turned up near my table and said, "Ma'am you seem new to this place" to which I replied "Yes and asked who are you?" "We make and sell tea at some of the top corporate brand's offices in this area." "I am Rajesh, a workman at Krishna Tea Flavors. I said, "ok." He further asked, "Ma'am which tea would you prefer, we have varieties from green and blue tea to iced tea." So, I said, "I would like to have a black tea" As I read it has more antioxidant properties than many others and moreover, I like its taste.

After finishing the tea, I prepared a presentation of some of the ideas that we can include in our marketing efforts. It was 1 PM. "Swati, its lunch time" come along with us." I said, "I have not bought the lunch today as I was feeling a bit unwell during the morning hours." "No problem, we have a cafeteria spread across the entire 3rd floor, we can have anything that we want from the coupon of 250 provided every day by our company." I felt elated and thought that it was a wonderful initiative for the employee's welfare. I had chole rice and 2 chapati's along with the salad and would say it was indeed good not only in terms of taste but also because fewer spices were added.

After lunch, we went downstairs to the open garden to discuss over the organization's culture and expectations. "They expect you to produce results," said Rakesh who was 2 years old in this organization and the rest we quite new, not more than one year old to this organization. Since we were handling the social media marketing division, we were to design unique ads for different platforms like Facebook, Instagram, Twitter etc. "For about half an hour we discussed about what trends are currently going on in social and digital media and then reached our cabins at around 2 PM.

It was almost time for the meeting, which was to happen in the board room. "Come in all," said Mr. Ravikant Verma, who was our reporting manager. Apart from Mr. Verma, there was Mr. Shyam Sehgal who was the digital media head. "What all have you worked on?" and "What all is currently practised by our organization"? asked Mr. Verma. I said, "Sir our organization is strongly present in all the platforms except Quora and Twitter, I think we can work on this to build our presence across all the platforms." "Ok, but then we also have to work better on the current platforms," said Mr. Verma.

"Do you want to add any point regarding the existing platforms?" I said, "Sir, our reach through Facebook reach is not that much, maybe because of the less effective keywords." It seemed he was in a hurry to take other members' suggestions and asked, "Aman and Rakesh, what do you think about this?" Rakesh said, "It may be also due to the type of content that we create, we can work on that aspect also." "Just work on content as of now," Rakesh and Aman, you may present your presentation as well." I enthusiastically said, "Sir, can I also present?" to which he replied, "Maybe in the next meeting." I did not understand why this was happening.

Rakesh presented his part and then Aman continued and they both were lauded for this. "We will work on the entire content part now and will work immensely on influencer marketing." Rakesh and Aman, you take the lead and Rashi and Swati, you all can work together." It had almost been 8 months in the organization and was not getting any acknowledgement for the work that was done on my part. I finally decided to meet my manager. His cabin was in the form of a semi-circle, and on the round side was his chair fit in a manner that gave a look of the half-moon. I took the permission before entering and he said, "Come in Swati."

I sat on a couch placed nearby and asked, "There is something that is continuously disturbing me and I feel my efforts towards the development of the organization are going in vain." He asked, "Swati, you all are working with each other then what is the issue?" "Sir, mine and Rashi's suggestions are always kept secondary and sometimes ignored," I said. To which he replied, "They both are experienced in this organization and you two are comparatively new. So, it will take time," So asked, "time for what?" "Let's go for a cup of coffee" and discuss on what you need to improve so that your points can be considered." I was shocked and broken and wanted to complain to the upper HR Grievances division but did not have proof so decided to wait for some more time. I agreed to the cafeteria visit and planned that once I visited, I would record everything that he said on the video recorder.

He met me in the cafeteria, and we started having a conversation. "It's a beautiful place, right?" I said, "Sir, you called me up here to tell me about my weak points that I can work on, right?" He said, "Swati, do you know, you are quite smarter than all other people that I have ever worked with in life. I want you to go very far in life but men will be men." I understood his psychology and asked, do you think men are superior then women" He said, "It's a society designed in that way." I decided to give my resignation naming him being the reason.

Never stop believing in what you have always dreamed of. With good deeds and sheer hard work, dreams do come true. Remember, you have a higher purpose in life (i.e. is the growth of the entire human race)